Reach Education, Inc. | Washington, DC

Reach: Books by Teens
Published by
Reach Education, Inc.
www.reachincorporated.org

ISBN: 0996927468
ISBN-13: 978-0996927468

DEDICATION

This book is dedicated to any kid
who is going through some
troubles or problems or sadness.
We want you to know that
you are not alone.

Late one evening, a camel finds himself inside a dark, lonely crate.
The crate starts rocking back and forth on the waves.
It's pitch black and he hears strange sounds surrounding him. He has no room to move and it's so humid that he gasps for breath.
His seasickness and fear causes him to enter into a deep sleep.

Hours later the camel awakens into a whole new world.

He slowly opens his eyes, one eye at a time.

He's no longer in the dark, tiny crate. The sun shines in his face. He sees fresh green grass and crowds of people passing by.

He's startled by the *whinny whinny whinny* of a horse nearby and he starts to panic.

His first reaction is to run, but he sees all the guards surrounding him.

"Where am I?" yells the camel. "What am I doing here?"

"You're in the Smithsonian Zoo," explains a nearby squirrel, chomping on a nut.

"What's a zoo?" asks the confused camel.

Before the squirrel can answer, a zookeeper shouts,

"Lunch time! Come get your food!"

On his way to the food,
the camel sees a strange,
enormous animal.

This creature looks strong and mighty, but he's also got dreads that hang past his ears, he's wearing dark sunglasses, and he's moonwalking and singing "Do You Remember the Time" by Michael Jackson.

The camel isn't too sure about this strange, enormous animal. He's never seen anything like it, but he thinks it may be a hippo.

Before he can even start eating his lunch, the hippo starts walking towards him.

"Why the long face?" asks the hippo.

The camel doesn't know what to say. He's afraid to tell this strange creature the truth: he doesn't know where he is, he wants to go home, and he misses his family.

Before he can say a word, the hippo asks,
"Come on man,
What's your name?
Where are you from?
Where's your family?"

The camel takes a deep breath.
"My name's Larry. I'm from Egypt."
He lowers his head and softly murmurs,
"My family died in a sandstorm."

"What?" the hippo asks.
"I didn't hear that last part."

Larry is too sad and timid to say it again.
"Nevermind," he says.

"Lunch is over!" shouts the zookeeper.

The hippo puts his big, heavy hand on
Larry's hump and says,
"Well, anyway, welcome.
My name's Tunechi."

The next morning, Larry is up and ready for a new day. As he gets ready, he starts to spit a rhyme and make a beat.

Larry loves to rap. He does it every free minute he gets. Rapping is the only way Larry can express himself. It comforts him when he's sad.

Tunechi walks up to Larry with his eyebrows raised and a huge grin on his face.

He exclaims, "I can't believe you can rap!"
And in his excitable way he asks,
"How long have been rapping?
What's your form of rapping?
Has anyone else heard you rap?"

Larry's startled by Tunechi. He didn't know anyone else was listening and he doesn't want anyone to know his whole story.

Also, the hippo's constant questioning makes him nervous.

So Larry moves away from Tunechi without answering any of his questions.

"Hey listen!" Tunechi yells after him. "There's a talent show tomorrow and you should definitely do it."

Larry continues to walk away. He's thinking about his rap and about how the other animals would react to his story.

"You're really, really good!" Tunechi yells.

"We can do it together, we'll be a duo. What do you think about that, you in or you out?" Tunechi asks.

Larry stops walking.

He realizes that if Tunechi likes his rapping, then the other animals might like it too.

So, with a great sigh and lot of hesitation, Larry responds, "Fine, I'll do it."

"Cool! It's tomorrow after the zoo closes. Don't be late!" Tunechi declares with uncontrollable excitement.

All that night, Larry paces back and forth. He's still worried about the rest of the zoo animals hearing his story.

Everyone here seems so confident and comfortable. They don't seem like they have any cares in the world, especially Tunechi.

He thinks they won't understand his problems and that they'll say he doesn't belong.

What if the other animals boo him off the stage and make fun of him?

BOOOOO!!
BOOOOO!!!
BOOOOOOOO!!!

Larry stays up almost all night worrying.

When morning finally comes, he is really really nervous, but he starts getting ready anyway.

All day he practices his rap in his head, but he tells himself he still might not do it.

Later in the day,
once the zoo has
closed, Larry finds
himself backstage at
the talent show,
peeping through the
curtains.

He can see a large
crowd of animals
and again he gets
really, really
nervous.

Tunechi walks up to Larry and is ready to go
on stage.

"All right, Larry, we're ready! I'm about to
get the crowd warmed up for us," says
Tunechi excitedly.

Tunechi starts moonwalking onto the stage singing "Smooth Criminal" by Michael Jackson.

Fog starts to come up from beneath the platform and there are bright, colorful lights dancing across the stage.

The crowd starts going wild, roaring and squawking. Elephants wave their trunks from side to side.

ANNIE
ARE
YOU

Tunechi's still singing and now it's Larry's turn to join him. As Larry walks onto the stage, the smoke clears out and the spotlight shines upon him.

The crowd goes still and all you can hear is crickets chirping.

Larry freezes and blanks.

He turns around as if he's about to walk off-stage. But before he can leave, Tunechi starts to introduce him.

"Yo everybody, this is my man Larry!
He came all the way from Egypt.
Give it up for him!"
The crowd slowly starts chanting,
"Larr-y, Larr-y, Larr-y!"
Larr-y ...
Larr-y ...
Larr-y ..
LARR-

Larry's knees start to buckle, but he looks into the crowd and sees all the excited faces. He closes his eyes and starts to spit his rhyme.

My name is Larry
Got three humps on my back
My family died in a sand attack
And to this day I still have flashbacks
I was kidnapped from Egypt, forced in a shack,
Trapped in this tight space, it was cold and black
I was hungry for days, there weren't any snacks
Now I'm stuck at this zoo, which is really whack
I miss my family and my red Pontiac

I miss the beautiful
pyramids resting in the sun,
Making happy faces,
just having fun

I miss playing tug of war
with my friends,
Stuck at some zoo is not
what I imagined

All I think about is
what a life I had
Making new friends makes
me feel glad
But on the inside I still feel...
sad

At first no one moves, and Larry thinks maybe he has said too much.

But then all of a sudden the crowd goes wild, and Larry and Tunechi walk off the stage together.

All the animals crowd around them shouting out different stories.

A lion roars, "I feel you, Larry, my mother was killed when I was just a cub."

A monkey screeches, "I understand, I was taken from Indonesia."

And a parrot squawks, "I was taken from Costa Rica to be sold as a pet."

Larry is taken aback by all the stories that are similar to his. He realizes that he's not alone and that the other zoo animals can understand his very sad story. Because, as it turns out, they all have sad stories too.

Even Tunechi looks sad for a moment.

"You OK?" Larry asks Tunechi, leaning down close to whisper in his ear.

"Yeah, man. You just move a brother. I miss my Mama sometimes is all," replies Tunechi.

Larry can't believe it. Even singing, laughing, moonwalking Tunechi has problems.

Tunechi continues, "Anyway, welcome to the family and your new home."

As they're walking away from the stage, the crowd begins to cheer loudly.

"Encore! Encore! Encore!"

Tunechi nods his head in approval. "Are you ready for this?" he asks Larry.

Larry smiles and does a little Harlem Shake.

"Let's do this."

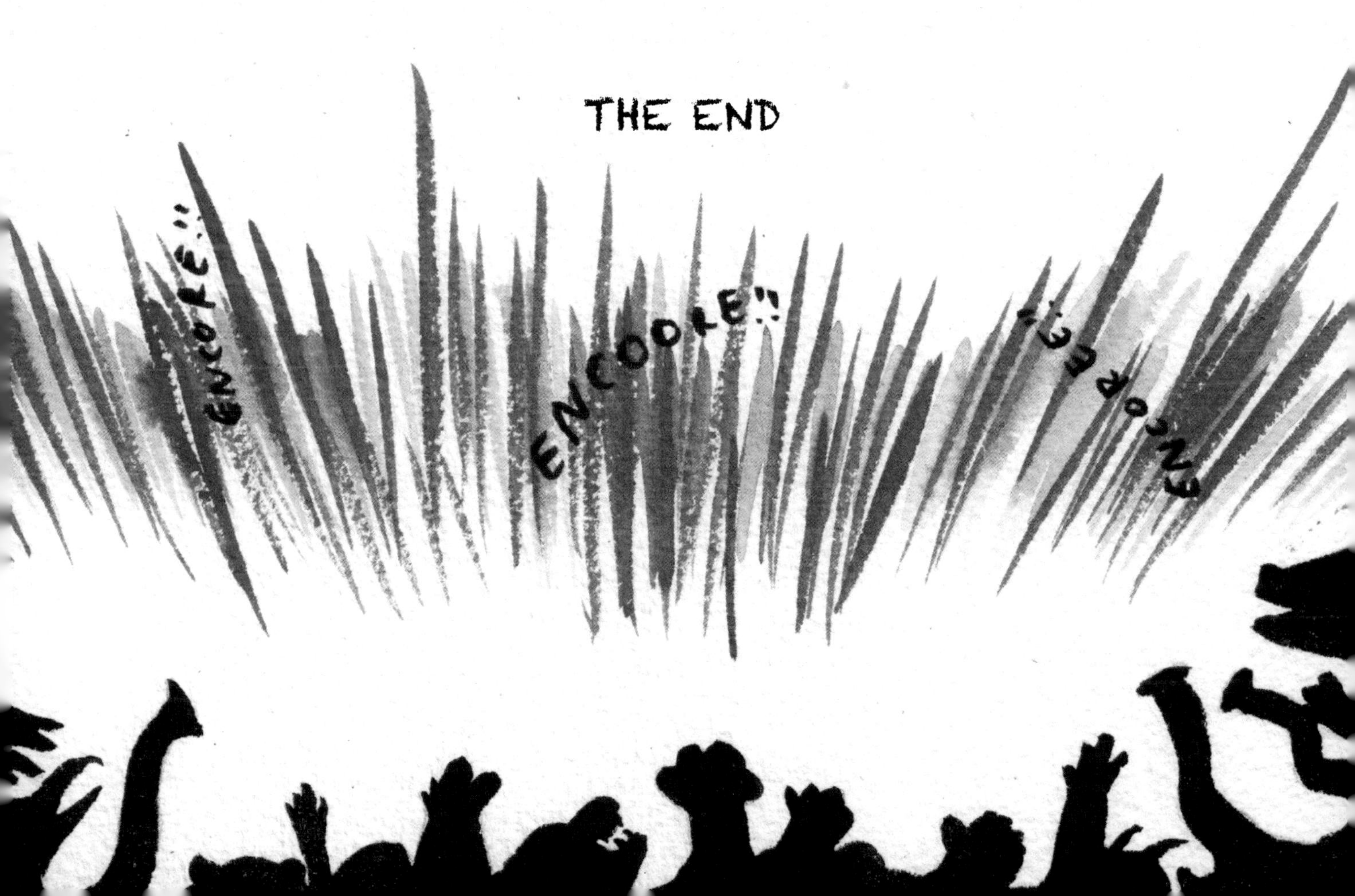

Acknowledgments

In July 2013, fifteen students embarked on an exciting journey. Tasked with creating original children's books, these young people brainstormed ideas, generated potential plots, wrote, revised, and provided critiques. In the end, four amazing books were created, showing again what teenagers can do when their potential is unleashed with purpose. Our fifteen authors have our immense gratitude and respect: Joshua, Jordan, Rashaan, Za'Metria, Marc, Sasha, Dana, Rico, Sejal, Angelo, Sean, Brandon, DaQuan, Kyare, and Zorita.

We also appreciate the leadership provided by our instructional leaders: Kaitlyn Denzler, Andrea Mirviss, and Brian Ovalles. Jusna Perrin, in addition to leading a team of teen writers, steered our summer program ship, seemingly with ease.

We also owe great thanks to our talented illustrators, Lucia Liu and Mira Ko, whose beautiful drawings brought these stories to life. And, most of all, we thank our dedicated and inspiring writing coach, Kathy Crutcher, who led our teens from the excitement of brainstorming through the hard work of revision to make these stories the best they can be.

Once the books were finished, publication costs could have made it difficult to share these stories with the world, so we appreciate the financial support provided by the New York Avenue Presbyterian Church, the Carr Family, the Denzler Family, Helen Runnells DuBois, the Hollowell Family, the Mirviss Family, and Cheryl Zabinski.

Most of all, we thank those of you who have purchased the books. We hope the smiles created as you read match those expressed as we wrote.

About the Authors

Rashaan Edwards likes to sing, rap, and write poetry. In his spare time he plays football and basketball. He is the brother of five and attends Eastern Senior High School.

Sejal Mobley is 16 years old and attends Perry Street Preparatory Public Charter School. Her hobbies include playing rugby, cheerleading, reading, and writing.

About the Authors

DaQuan Smith is a rising senior at Perry Street Preparatory Public Charter School. He's been practicing Islam for almost five years now and has been looked at differently for this choice. But he thinks being different could be the best thing ever: "Just be yourself and you'll find similarities in any person you come across."

Zorita Workman is 15 years old and enjoys making raps. She attends Perry Street Preparatory Public Charter School.

About the Illustrator

Lucia Liu is a sophomore at VCUarts, majoring in Painting & Printmaking and minoring in Creative Entrepreneurship. She has experience in fine art, art education, studio assisting, and illustration. In addition to art, she loves playing music and has participated in musical ensembles as a violinist for nearly ten years. More of her work can be found at lucialiu.wix.com/artportfolio.

About the Story Coach

Kathy Crutcher has mentored young writers since 2003 and is passionate about empowering others to tell their stories. She has led fiction, memoir, and playwriting workshops for writers ages 8-18 and has also taught writing at the university level. Her students have won national recognition through the Scholastic Writing Awards and have been published both nationally and locally. To learn more about Kathy's mentoring, editing, and publishing projects, visit www.kathycrutcher.com.

About Reach Incorporated

Reach Incorporated develops confident grade-level readers and capable leaders by training teens to teach, creating academic benefit for all involved.

Founded in 2009, Reach recruits entering 9th grade students to be elementary school tutors. Elementary school students average 1.5 grade levels of reading growth per year of participation. This growth — equal to that created by highly effective teachers — is created by high school students who average more than two grade levels of growth per year of program participation.

Reach creates readers. Reach creates leaders. And, by lifting two populations through a uniquely structured relationship, Reach is effectively attacking Washington DC's literacy crisis.

During the summer of 2013, Reach launched a new program to build on school-year gains made by program tutors. As part of this program, teens partnered with professional writers and illustrators to create original children's stories. These stories, written entirely by our teens, provide our young people with the opportunity to share their talents and creativity with a wider audience.

By purchasing our books, you support student-led, community-driven efforts to improve educational outcomes in the District of Columbia.

Learn more at www.reachincorporated.org.

Made in the USA
Coppell, TX
21 February 2024